We Sing the City

By
Mary Beth Lundgren

Illustrated by
Donna Perrone

Clarion Books • New York

Clarion Books
a Houghton Mifflin Company imprint
215 Park Avenue South, New York, NY 10003
Text copyright © 1997 by Mary Beth Lundgren
Illustrations copyright © 1997 by Donna Perrone

Illustrations executed in oil pastels and
colored pencil on blue Canson paper.
Type is set in 16/20 Cantoria.

For information about this and other Houghton Mifflin trade and reference books
and multimedia products, visit The Bookstore at Houghton Mifflin on
the World Wide Web at (http://www.hmco.com/trade/).

Printed in the U.S.A.

Library of Congress Cataloging-in-Publication Data

Lundgren, Mary Beth.
We sing the city / by Mary Beth Lundgren ;
illustrated by Donna Perrone.
p.   cm.
Summary: An ethnically diverse mixed group of children
describe all the wonderful diversity of the city where they live.
ISBN 0-395-68188-X
[1. City and town life—Fiction.]   I. Perrone, Donna, ill.   II. Title.
PZ7.L978848We   1997   93-34860
CIP
AC

WOZ   10 9 8 7 6 5 4 3 2 1

To Ted—my dance partner—for the beat.
To Lila, Susan, and Nina, for the harmony and grace notes.
And to children the world over, for their song.
—M. B. L.

To Mark, the love of my life,

so amazing . . . so strong.

He reached for the light

and he lives.

—D. P.

We Sing the City

We are:
Borisav, Brian, Carlos, Carol,
Faisal, Fernando, Akiri,
Nyla-Jean, White Wolf, Jackie, and Yitzhak;
Hisham, Muhamet, Haniya,
Wang, Nicholasa, Lech, and Natasha;
Saroj, Moosa, and Minh.
We are the children of the city.
WE SING.

We rock, roll, stroll, we shop
at the drugstore, hardware, Joe's shoe repair,
beauty salon, barber, Middle East market,
baker, butcher, candy shop.
We hunt for new school sneaks or birthday gifts

8

at downtown stores or at the mall.
Ummmmmmm—cashews roasting, french fries frying,
smell the cinnamon from the bakery buns.
Ahhhhhh—chocolate and coffee from faraway places.
We breathe in deeply and cheer.

Natasha's great-great-great-grandfather sailed from Siberia;
Nyla-Jean's walked from down south.
Great-grandfather White Wolf rode from the mountains,
as steel mills turned the sky red.
Bricklayers, stonemasons, carpenters built
houses, big porches, banks with fat pillars;
gargoyles grinned from each roof.
Brian's grandfather lettered hatbands;
Natasha's cobbled shoes.
Each neighborhood grew,
overlapped, spilled together.
Now the buildings bump the sky.
Today we sing our ancestors.

We sing of families,
eighth notes, half notes, whole notes.
We harmonize and improvise:
mother, father, boy, and girl;
grandpa, father, son;
mother, children, mom's best friend;
adopted kids, birth kids, shared kids,
stepfather, foster mother.
Blended together, we sing.

We fly high, soar, color the city with living:
above stores and under shops, by railroad tracks and bridges;
behind malls, beside walls, near highways, lakes, and rivers;
Germantown, Chinatown, New Saigon,
Slavic Village, Warehouse District, Little Tehran,
uptown, downtown,
east side, west side.
We sing of living in the city.

We test tones,
croon tunes,
talk tap.
We boogie with our friends who live and work in the city.
Women with signs picket on the corner,
kids spray-paint murals on dusty brick walls.

Policewoman, fireman, sanitation worker,
construction foreman, street cleaner, telephone repairman;
flower vendor, produce seller, electric meter reader,
and a sight-impaired man with his dog.
Accompanied, we serenade
our neighborhood.

We sing,
hustle horns, pound drums—
BAM! BAM!
We call out the birds:
seagulls, starlings, and sparrows;
cardinals, robins, and wrens;
blue jays, pigeons, and finches;
mourning doves, grackles, and crows.
Chitter, CHUCK, CHUCK,
chirp, cheep, peep,
CAW, CAW, coooooo, cooooooo.
Sometimes we feed them.

We cheer the animals:
some—elephants, tigers, giraffes, and gorillas;
polar bears, peacocks, piranhas—
that live in the zoo;
our dogs, cats, and gerbils; birds and white mice;
rabbits, hamsters, and snakes;
field mice and 'possums in vacant lots;
squirrels in trees,
moles underground,
raccoons in sewers and down by the river
that raid garbage cans late at night.
Crash. BANG!

17

We tap,
rap rhythms,
the flavors of the city.
We eat:
hotdogs, pizza, yogurt, sushi,

pasta, scones, and ice cream cones;
bagels and lox, greens and hamhocks,
tabouleh, couscous, black beans and rice,
baklava, burritos, and borscht.
We applaud the flavors of the city.

We scat scales, ring bells,
at Lakeridge Prep, St. Joe Academy,
Christian, parish, and Islamic schools,
home schools, Hebrew schools, daycare centers,
Amelia Erhardt Elementary,
or P.S. number 9.
We learn of life and roar our song.

YAYYY!
We shout, we sing,
our love of the city.
We are:
Borisav, Brian, Carlos, Carol,
Faisal, Fernando, Akiri,
Nyla-Jean, White Wolf, Jackie, and Yitzhak;
Hisham, Muhamet, Haniya,
Wang, Nicholasa, Lech, and Natasha;
Saroj, Moosa, and Mihn.

Ahmed, Ahn, Tony, and Ben moved in today.
New voices,
harmonies, melodies, sounds,
new music for the song
we sing.

We Sing the City